Ravenous Ralphie

by

Julie Brinckloe

Illustrated by Beth Budra

Ravenous Ralphie is one of the stories in the FastForWord® Bookshelf series of print and CD-ROM storybooks.

For more information on other products from Scientific Learning, visit www.scientificlearning.com.

Fast ForWord® Bookshelf is a registered tradmark of Scientific Learning Corporation.

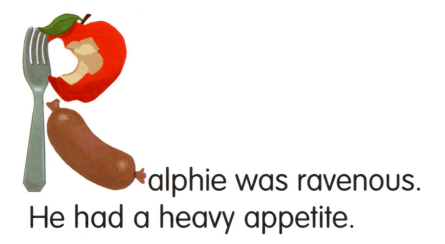

alphie was ravenous.
He had a heavy appetite.

Always ate all his food.
Every bite. Every bite.

3

Time for dinner.
Never late.

After dinner, clean plate.

Ravenous Ralphie ate and ate.
Ate and ate.

At the table, Ralphie said,
"Pass the jam, pass the bread."

"Pass the ham, pass the peas.
More, please! More, please!"

Table bare.
Don't care.
Ralphie ate the silverware.

Mama cried, "Ralphie, wait!"

Ralphie ate his dinner plate.

Ate the cup. Ate the spoon.
Ralphie ate all afternoon.

Time for supper, time to eat.
"Pass the muffins, pass the meat."

"Pass the beans, pass the cheese.
More, please! More, please!"

Time for bath, time for bed.
Ralphie'd rather eat, instead.

'Crunch, crunch—'
"What's that noise?"

"Ralphie's eating all his toys!"

"All his shoes, all his socks!
All his wooden building blocks!"

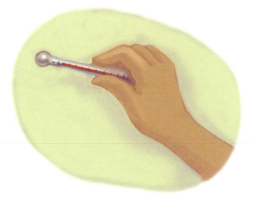

"Call the doctor! Call him quick!
Ralphie must be really sick!"

Papa cried, "No dial tone!
Ralphie ate the telephone!"

"Ate the cord, ate the plug.
Now he's chewing on the rug!"

Ralphie nibbled
down
the
stairs.

Ate the table, ate the chairs.

Every shelf and every book.

Every picture, every hook.

He chewed the china into bits.

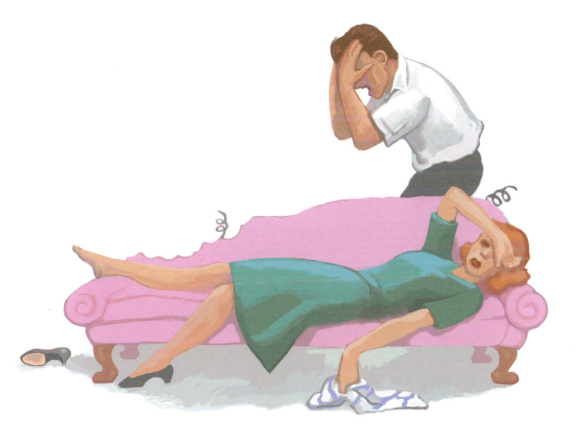

(Ma and Pa were having fits!)

Chewed up everything he found—

Chewed the house…to the ground!

Mama, Papa couldn't stay.
Took the boy and drove away.

But they didn't travel far—

Ralphie gobbled up the car!

Ate the road right up the hill.

Ralphie might be eating *still,*
but suddenly, a *lucky break!*—

Ralphie got a tummy ache.

The End